Published by Sourcebooks Jabberwocky,
an imprint of Sourcebooks, Inc.
P.O. Box 4410, Naperville, Illinois 60567-4410
(630) 961-3900
Fax: (630) 961-2168
www.jabberwockykids.com

Originally published in 2014 in the
United Kingdom by Macmillan
Children's Books, an imprint of
Macmillan Publishers Limited.

Library of Congress Cataloging-
in-Publication data is on
file with the publisher.

Printed and bound
in China.

10 9 8 7 6 5 4 3 2 1

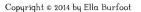

dedicated to
Mr Peershouse and the
noodle dragon

How to BAKE -a- BŌŌK

Ella Burfoot

sourcebooks
jabberwocky

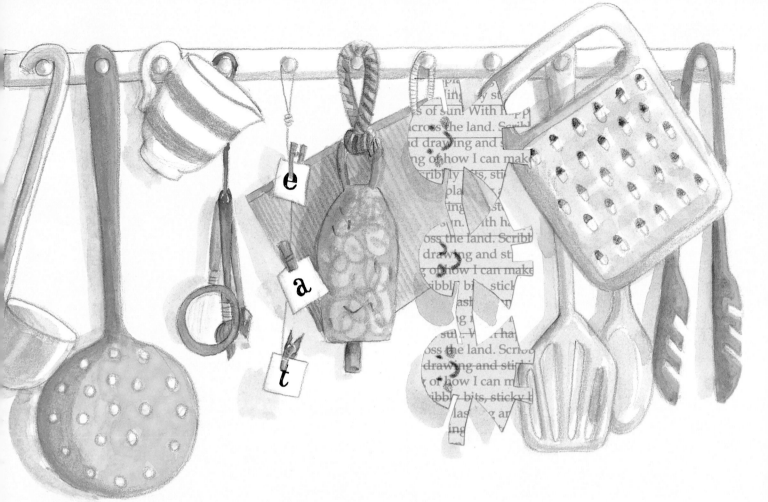

I am going to bake a book!

I'll break some ideas into a cup.

I'll beat them, whisk them, mix them up.

I'll weigh out the words—
just enough.

small
words

BIG
WORDS

MIXED
WORDS

Choosing the right
ones can be tough!

The small ones go into the pot,

HE, SHE, IT, WHEN,

and

WHAT.

I'll drop some big words from way up,

ELEPHANT,

CROCODILE,

BUTTERCUP!

COOKING FOR CREATIVES

AWFUL AUTHORS AND TERRIB

Fairy Cakes an

TASTY TAL

WOLF IT DOWN   by B.

GOLDILOCK

FANTASY
FUDGE   and

The Princess ar

EC

CA

Now that my story has begun,

I'll cut out characters, one by one.

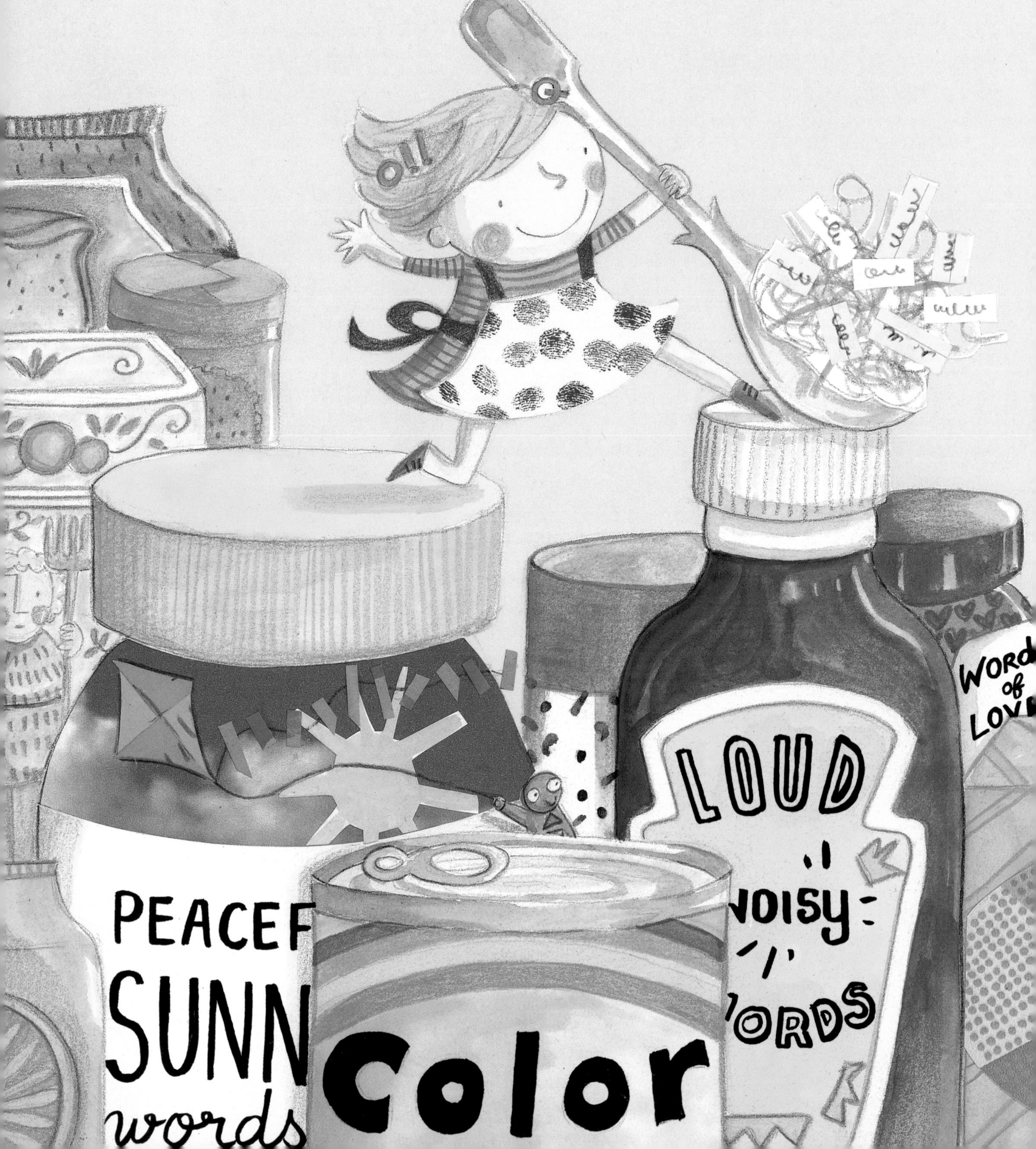
oi!
PEACEF
SUNN
words
Color
LOUD
NOISY
ORDS
Word
of
LOVE

Feelings, colors, sounds, a picture,
all add flavor to my mixture!

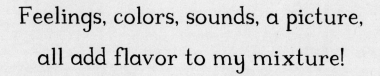

Giggly Word Jelly

ZAP MA WO

Sad Words

I'll add a watery word or two.

I'll pour them in and stir them through.

Splish, splosh, splash, drip, or sprinkle.

Glug and gurgle, squelch and twinkle.

Now I'll put a lid on it.

Wait a while.

Let it sit.

It's not until I roll it out,

that I'll find out what it's all about!

And now I'll lay it in the tin,

so my characters can all jump in!

Next, the middle,
   the action, the filling!
Into the pan,
   without any spilling.

Now all I'll do
   is simply add
a spoonful of good
   and a pinch of bad.

Turn up the heat—
   the bubbles quicken.
And then my plot
   begins to thicken.

PERIODS

CAPITAL LET

Dried
Princess Peas

Each sentence
   will taste much better
if I add periods
   and capital letters.
I'll find them in a moment...
   I've seen them myself...
Here they are!
   Big cupboard, top shelf.

STORY POPS

Porridge
Oats

GIANT
TURNIP
Slices

Finally the ending—I'll press it down,
and add decorations all around.

I will glaze it with happiness,
leave it to cook,

Then bake it, brown it,
and finish my book!

I turn the pages and I can see
that my recipe has turned out tasty.
I've done everything as the cook...

...to make my story a delicious book!